THE IRON NEEDLE

Amanda Harvey

Lothrop, Lee & Shepard Books
New York

For my mother
and for Selahattin Şimşek

Printed in Hong Kong

First U.S. Edition   1   2   3   4   5   6   7   8   9   10

Library of Congress Cataloging in Publication Data was not available in time for
publication of this book, but can be obtained from the Library of Congress.
ISBN 0-688-13192-1. Library of Congress Catalog Card Number 93-32679

Elizabeth had lost her needle. It had fallen between
the cracks in the floor.

Her mother didn't have another one.

Neither did Mr. Heath at the shop. "You'll have to
go down to the foundry and make one," he said.

The iron foundry was at the foot of the hill, where
it smoked and roared all day long.

"Hello there, young Elizabeth!" called Mr. Furnival, (who lived on the next block). "Come to give us a hand?"

"Just for this afternoon," Elizabeth told him as Mr. Furnival, with hands as rough as sandpaper, tied his apron around her, gave her his hat, and pointed her toward the furnace room.

The molten iron rushed out

and cooled on the sand.

"Pull that door!" – Push that trolley!" – she heard
the furnace men shout.

"Steady, steady!" they cried, as she wrestled with
the iron under the hammer.

The man on the rolling mill measured a length of iron for her. "We'll nip it off here, shall we?"

At lunchtime, the foundry workers shared their
sandwiches. Mr. Furnival poured her a cup of tea
while telling her about the gooseberries he was
growing for the fruit show.

Then she took her iron bar to the blacksmith,

who sang as she worked:

For my tiger bold I made a chain,
I filed the iron so smooth and plain,
For my gentle horse I made a shoe –
I beat the iron and hammered it true.

and Elizabeth replied:

In my needle sharp I'll put an eye.

Through the hole I'll see the sky.

And Elizabeth, home again, finished her sewing.